The ADVENTURES of DUDE REMY

a four-book collection

Copyright Registration and Date:
TXu002192779/2020-02-27

Print ISBN: 978-1-66782-6-776

The ADVENTURES of DUDE REMY

a four-book collection

written by
MICHELE ROBIN

illustrated by
VICTOR TAVARES

BOOK ONE

OFF THE LINE

I'm a tough pickup truck on the lot to be sold,
My shiny black paint
makes me feel rather bold.

Made for construction and hauling stuff,
A family just bought me, oddly enough.

Why would they want a rugged pickup truck?

I can't decide if this is good or bad luck.

I have two doors, a short flatbed, and my engine's a Hemi,

Did I hear them just say they'll call me Dude Remy?

On Clay's sixteenth birthday, I realize why his parents chose me;
He's getting his driver's license at the DMV.

A two-person cab, for a teenager, is just the right fit.

Peace of mind for his parents,
only one passenger can sit.

Day after day, Clay drives me to school,
I'm feeling self-conscious,
but he's feeling cool.

12

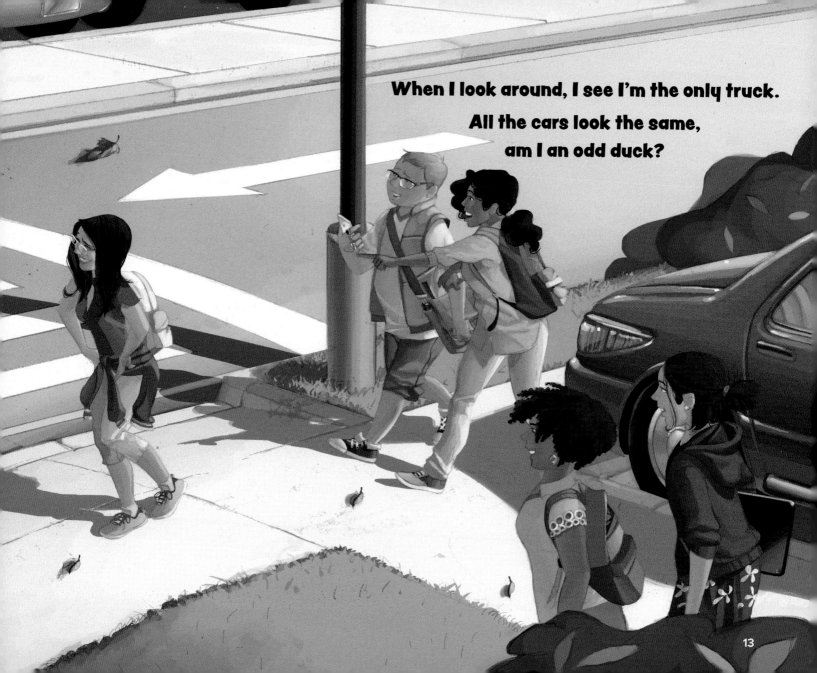

When I look around, I see I'm the only truck.
All the cars look the same,
am I an odd duck?

13

In the high school parking lot,
the cars all glare,
I do not fit in; I'm alone and scared.

By the students' reactions,
I feel more than okay,
Which means, the growth of my confidence is underway.

When this school day ends, it's not the same,
We're off to the rink for tonight's hockey game.

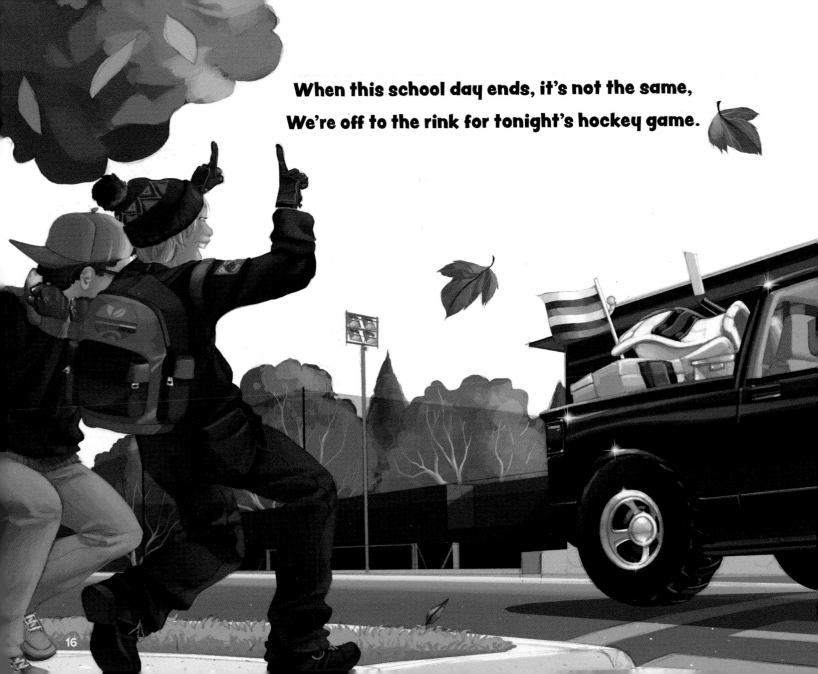

Hauling Clay's goalie equipment way back in the bed,
The kids line the street, cheering for a victory ahead.

17

We pull up to the ice rink as the weather turns cold,
I watch the game through the window;
it never gets old.

As spring comes around, it is baseball time,
Watching Clay from the side, down the third-base line.

It was my lucky day
when this family bought me;
I can't imagine where else I would be.

It's not every day a truck like me has a boy,
Who loves me as much as his childhood toy!

BOOK TWO

THE UPS AND DOWNS

Graduation from high school is the big event of the day,

Clay leaves for college,
which means he is moving away.

Will I just sit in the driveway day after day?

Just parked there alone, no adventures or play?

25

The summer was fun, now it's time for goodbyes.
Clay turns to see me with tears in his eyes.

My headlights dim as I watch them pull out,
I'm feeling bad for myself, I can't help but pout.

After moments of silence, I hear footsteps all over the place,
Spencer rushes from the garage, a giant smile on his face.

Loaded up with his football gear,
And just like that, I'm off to cheer!

We arrive at the stadium,
there's a giant crowd,
This could be fun, it's really loud!

When the game is over, the players can't wait,
To climb in the back, it's time to celebrate.

At home the next day,
Spencer cleans my inside,
My life is amazing,
I'm enjoying the ride.

Hanging out with Spence fills the void left by Clay.
Both brothers are fun in their own special way.

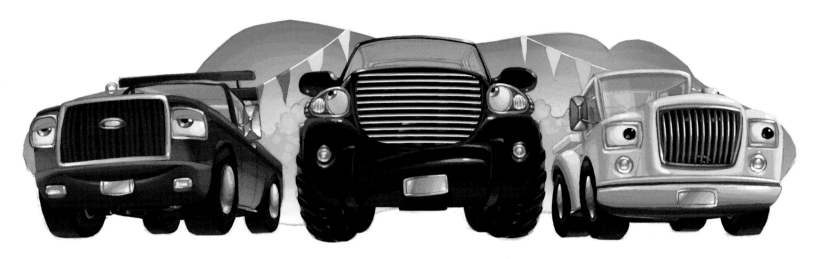

Having one buddy is great, but life is better with two,

With all their activities, I have plenty to do.

Looking back, I felt strange parked next to all cars,
Being unique makes me lucky, I am a star.

I stand out in the parking lot,
easy to see,
And I'm really happy,
just being me!

BOOK THREE

A DIFFERENT DIRECTION

The summer flew by as fast as before,
It's hard to believe Spencer's now out the door.

Another off to college, my other best bud,
I'm feeling sad, like I'm stuck in the mud.

It happens again, I'm alone and feeling blue,
But wait, what's that? Could it really be true?

42

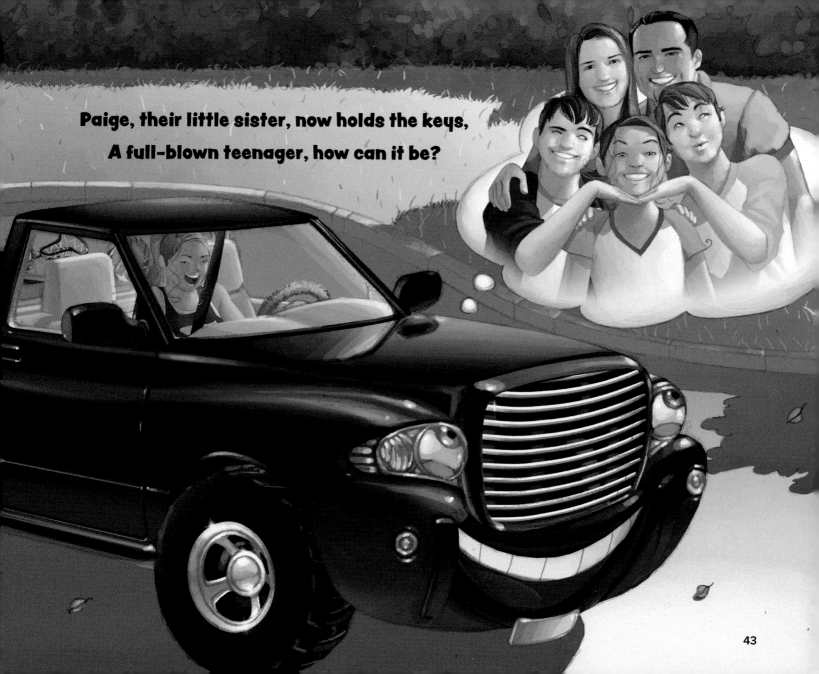

Paige, their little sister, now holds the keys,
A full-blown teenager, how can it be?

They talk about girl power, what does that mean?
I guess I'll find out with this super-cool teen.

My steering wheel's pink now,
it's fuzzy and chic,

For a pickup, I'm trendy, I see people peek.

45

The music is bubbly as Paige sings along,
I've never heard this kind of pop song.

We arrive at the field,
the lacrosse stick in back,
Along with tons of balloons
tied to my cargo rack.

A roar from the field, it's hard to ignore,

The girls are all screaming with that final score.

I can't help but feel a part of the team,
Warming my heart, my headlights beam.

Ever since Paige's brothers grew up to be men,
I never thought I could be this happy again.

It just goes to show you, some changes are good,
I wouldn't switch a thing, even if I could.

A new adventure today, I don't recognize this place,
I'm scared to pull in, my engine starts to race.

Slowly moving forward, at a cautious pace,
The brushes tickling my body, the sprayers washing my face.

The hot air blowers are like the wind in my grill,
An automatic carwash, this outing's a thrill!

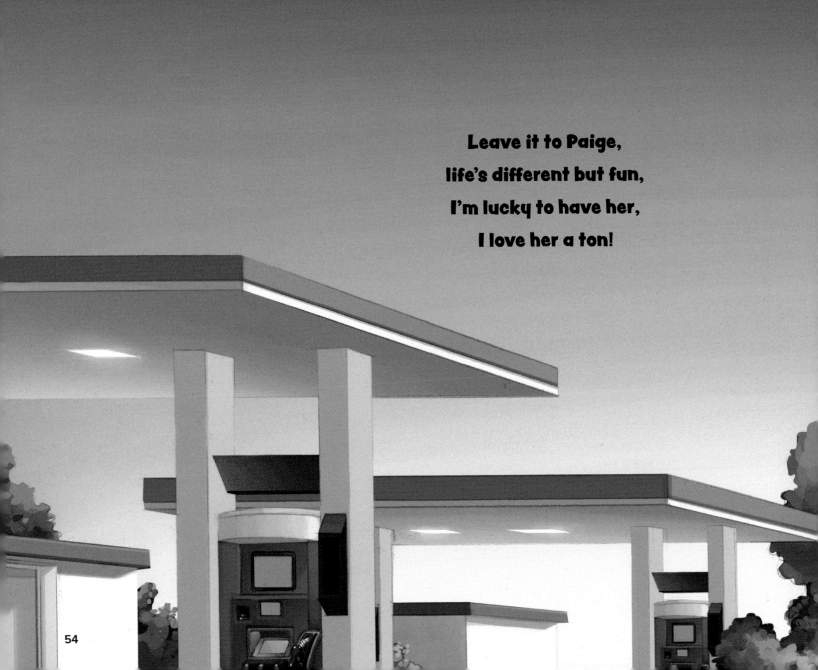

Leave it to Paige,
life's different but fun,
I'm lucky to have her,
I love her a ton!

54

BOOK FOUR

THE JOURNEY

We've arrived at the airport, it is now Paige's day,

She's off to college far, far away.

They exchange hugs and kisses with gigantic smiles,
I can see these goodbyes will take quite a while.

When Paige walks away, her mom starts to cry,

Hops in my cab, and pats her eyes dry.

As we leave the airport, she voices her pain,

She starts talking to me as if to explain,

"DUDE REMY, YOU KEPT THEM SAFE, DAY AND NIGHT,
RAIN, SLEET, OR SNOW, DARKNESS OR LIGHT.

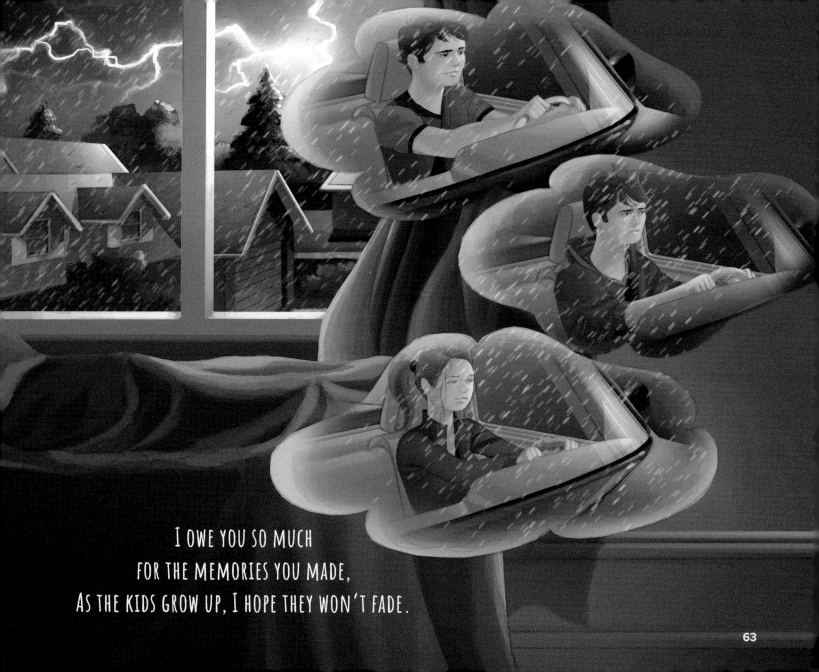

I OWE YOU SO MUCH
FOR THE MEMORIES YOU MADE,
AS THE KIDS GROW UP, I HOPE THEY WON'T FADE.

It's hard to imagine you put out to pasture,
But time keeps passing by faster and faster.

Your flatbed lays bare, no sports gear inside it,
It reminds me of home, which now is too quiet.

Heading out to the country, your surroundings will change,
Don't let that scare you, even if it feels strange.

Retiring you to the farm, our family retreat,
The kids will come visit, it's where we all meet."

The long journey is over, we are finally here,
"I have a surprise for you, Dude Remy, you'll see that we care.
Our old vintage truck, a friend we adore,
He's eagerly awaiting you, outside the barn door."

We head down the driveway, as we go through the gate,
"You'll meet Turquoise Charlie; I simply can't wait."

Looking awestruck at first, both trucks' headlights roam,
"Dude Remy, there'll be tons of hauling and loading;
you are finally home!"

To my Golden Goose, aka Papa Goose.

Thank you for making our dreams come true!

MICHELE ROBIN lives in Chicago with her husband, Craig and her spunky Bernese Mountain Dog, Bode. Michele's greatest achievement was raising their three kids, the loves of her life.

Family is Michele's number one priority and it's reflected in this children's book series. The Adventures of Dude Remy is Michele's legacy, and provides a window into the life her family grew up sharing. This story is filled with life lessons prompting parents to have discussions with their kids helping them to build confidence.